KT-570-038

Sophie Kinsella

Mummy Fairy and Me

Unicorn Wishes

Illustrations by Marta Kissi

PUFFIN

PUFFIN BOOKS

UK | USA | Canada | Ireland | Australia
India | New Zealand | South Africa

Puffin Books is part of the Penguin Random House group of companies
whose addresses can be found at global.penguinrandomhouse.com.

www.penguin.co.uk   www.puffin.co.uk   www.ladybird.co.uk

Aberdeenshire Council Libraries	
4011529	
Askews & Holts	01-Apr-2019
JF	£5.99
J	

The m

Text design by Mandy Norman
Printed in Great Britain by Clays Ltd, Elcograf S.p.A.

A CIP catalogue record for this book is available from the British Library

ISBN: 978–0–241–38026–0

All correspondence to:
Puffin Books
Penguin Random House Children's
80 Strand, London WC2R 0RL

MIX
Paper from
responsible sources
FSC® C018179
www.fsc.org

Penguin Random House is committed to a
sustainable future for our business, our readers
and our planet. This book is made from Forest
Stewardship Council® certified paper.

PUFFIN BOOKS

Mummy Fairy and Me

Unicorn Wishes

Read all the Mummy Fairy books
by Sophie Kinsella!

Mummy Fairy and Me

Mummy Fairy and Me:
Fairy-in-Waiting

Mummy Fairy and Me:
Unicorn Wishes

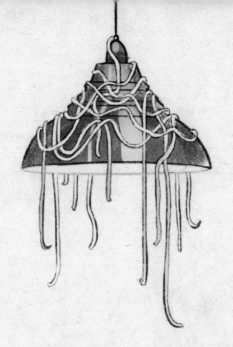

For Diggory

CONTENTS

Meet Mummy Fairy and me

Hello. I'm called Ella Brook and I live in a town called Cherrywood with my mummy, my daddy and my baby brother, Ollie.

My mummy looks normal, just like any other mummy . . . but she's not. Because she can turn into a fairy. All she has to do is stamp her feet three times, clap her hands, wiggle her bottom and say, 'Marshmallow' . . . and **POOF!** she's Mummy Fairy. Then if she says, 'Toffee apple,' she's just Mummy again.

My Aunty Jo and Granny are fairies too, because all the girls in my family turn into fairies when they grow up. They can all fly and turn invisible and do real magic. Mummy and Aunty Jo also have a really cool wand called a Computawand V5. It has magic powers, a computer screen, Fairy Apps, Fairy Mail and Fairy Games!

The problem is that Mummy is still not very good at doing magic spells, even though she works really hard at her lessons on FairyTube with her Fairy Tutor, Fairy Fenella. But one day she's going to get everything right.

When I'm grown up, I'll be a fairy like her too! Mummy calls me her Fairy-in-Waiting. I'll have big sparkly wings and my own beautiful shiny crown, and I'll be able to do magic just like Mummy. I already know what my first spell will be. I'll wish for a unicorn of my very own.

Although I can't do spells just yet, I can play with my magic wardrobe. You'll meet Wardrobe later.

Being a Fairy-in-Waiting is a big secret. I'm not allowed to tell anyone, not even my best friends, Tom and Lenka. And I definitely can't tell my Not-Best Friend, Zoe. She is the meanest girl ever and she lives next door. Sometimes I think she might find out about Mummy being a fairy.

But she hasn't yet. And life in a fairy family is fun! Even when there's a hitch or a glitch . . .

UPERIDOO!
The day we flew to school

It was time for school and we were going to be late. I knew this because Mummy was running around the house shouting, 'Where's my bag? Where's my bag?'

'I'll find it,' said Daddy. He looked under the table and in the fridge. 'Not here. Where did you see it last?'

'I don't know!' wailed Mummy. She threw all the sofa cushions on the floor, but her bag wasn't on the sofa. It wasn't in the microwave either.

I quickly looked in all the drawers. Ollie thought we were playing a game. He pointed at the ceiling and said, **'Weezi-weezi-weezi!'**

'All right,' said Mummy. 'There's nothing for it.' She stamped her feet three times, clapped her hands, wiggled her bottom and said, 'Marshmallow' . . . and **POOF!** she was a fairy. Then she

picked up her Computawand
from the table. Most of the time it
looks just like a normal phone, but as soon
as she touches it, the screen starts to glow
and it grows into a wand. Mummy says a
wand needs a fairy's touch to come alive.

Mummy Fairy waved her
Computawand, pressed a code
on the screen – *bleep-bleep-bloop*
– and said, '*Bageridoo!*'

Nothing happened.

I looked at Daddy, and Daddy looked
at me.

Mummy says when she was at school she was so busy doing sums and playing tennis and telling people what to do that she didn't have time to practise her spells properly. Granny says if only she used an old-fashioned wand instead of that silly Computawand, then her spells would work *much* better.

'I don't think the spell worked,' I said anxiously. 'Shall we just keep looking for the bag?'

'Well, it *should* have worked,' said Mummy Fairy. She bashed her Computawand.

'What's wrong with this thing?'

'Look,' said Daddy, and he pointed through the open window. 'What's that?'

We all peered out. There was a sort of multicoloured cloud in the sky. It was getting bigger and bigger.

'What *is* it?' said Mummy Fairy.

'It's coming towards us,' said Daddy.

'It's bags!' I said. 'It's lots of bags! It looks like it's going to rain bags.'

The cloud was right above us. It rustled and quivered. There was a tremble of thunder. Then . . .

Whoomph!

There was a bang and the
bags started raining down
all over the house and garden.
There were all sorts of bags.
There were handbags, carrier
bags and paper bags. There was
a tartan shopping trolley and
a unicorn rucksack and a pink
bag with a big black buckle.

'Ooh,' said Mummy Fairy.
'I like that one!'

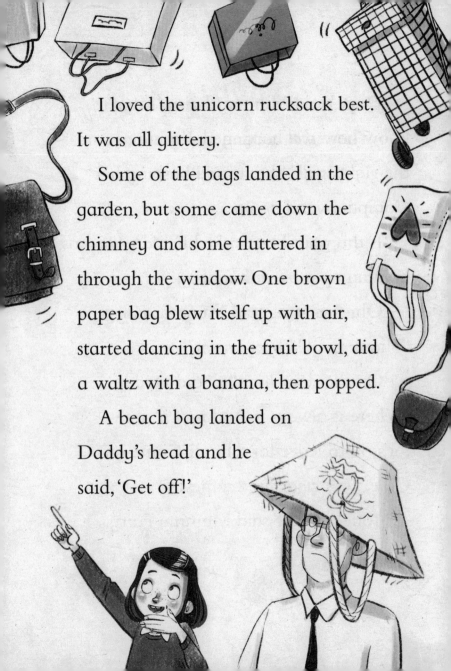

I loved the unicorn rucksack best. It was all glittery.

Some of the bags landed in the garden, but some came down the chimney and some fluttered in through the window. One brown paper bag blew itself up with air, started dancing in the fruit bowl, did a waltz with a banana, then popped.

A beach bag landed on Daddy's head and he said, 'Get off!'

'Oops,' said Mummy Fairy. 'I don't know how *that* happened. I'm sure I said the right spell.' She started bashing her Computawand again.

'Is this your bag?' asked Daddy. He was holding up a black handbag.

'Oh, *there* it is!' said Mummy Fairy. 'Thank you! Where was it?'

'On the door handle,' said Daddy. 'Where it always is. And isn't it time for you to leave for school? Come on, Ollie. Let's clear up the mess.'

'Toffee apple!' said Mummy Fairy.

And then she was just Mummy again.

★

I was getting worried because today was
a special Be on Time Day. Everyone
who came to school on time would get
a sticker from our teacher, Miss Amy.
The pupil who arrived first would get a
special shiny sticker. I really, really wanted
a shiny sticker. But it was already eight
o'clock. School starts at half past eight, so
we needed to get going.

'Quick, Mummy!' I said. **'*Quick!*'**

I ran out of the door, lugging my

school bag. Next door, my Not-Best
Friend Zoe and her mum were coming
out of their house. Zoe usually leaves
earlier than us because she does swimming
or ice skating before school. She is a very
busy girl.

I've known Zoe all my life, since we
were both babies in prams. Her mum
always says: 'Ella and Zoe are best friends!
They love each other!'

But she doesn't know how mean Zoe
is to me. She pinches me when no one's
looking. She says nasty things when

Miss Amy isn't around. And once she ripped my brand-new furry pencil case. On purpose.

'Morning, Ella!' said Zoe's mum, and got into her car.

Zoe turned round so her mum couldn't see her, then stuck out her tongue. 'You're going to be late!' she said. 'We're going to beat you! Loser! Bye-ee!' She laughed her horrible laugh, jumped in the car and slammed the door.

19

Their car started and roared off down the road.

'Mummy!' I yelled. **'*Come on!*'**

I really, *really* didn't want Zoe to get the shiny sticker.

At last we got in our car and set off.

Mummy said, 'Don't worry, Ella – we'll be there in no time! I'll drive super fast.'

But as we turned the corner we saw a traffic jam. Not just a little traffic jam but a GREAT BIG traffic jam. There were cars and buses and even a big lorry, all squashed together in the road.

'Oh dear,' said Mummy. 'I'm sure it will move soon.'

But it didn't. We sat there and sat there and nothing moved. Some cars started to hoot their horns. Other cars turned round to go a different way – but *we* couldn't go a different way. I was getting more and more worried.

'Don't worry,' said Mummy. 'I'm sure Miss Amy won't mind if you're late.'

'But I can't be late for school!' I wailed. 'I *can't*! Today is Be on Time Day! If we get to school on time, we get a sticker!'

'A sticker?' said Mummy.

'Yes, a sticker! And whoever arrives
first gets a special shiny sticker. And Zoe
will get there first, and she'll get the shiny
sticker and I won't.'

'A shiny sticker ...' Mummy
thought for a moment. 'Well,
that's different.'

She stamped her feet three times, clapped her hands, wiggled her bottom on the car seat and said, 'Marshmallow' . . . and **POOF!** she was a fairy.

Her shimmery wings were all squashed up in the car. I couldn't believe it. I said, 'Mummy Fairy, someone will see you!'

'No one's looking,' she said. 'Now, let's get out of this traffic jam.'

'How are we going to do that?' I asked.

'We're going to fly,' she said.

'Fly?' My eyes went wide. I had never flown in a car before.

'Of course! But first we need to be invisible.'

Mummy Fairy took her Computawand out of her bag. The screen started to glow and it grew into a wand. She pointed it at herself, me and the car, pressed a code on the screen – *bleep-bleep-bloop* –

and said, 'Inviseridoo!'

I felt a funny kind of tingling. 'Are we both invisible now?' I looked around. 'Is the car invisible too?'

'Yes.' Mummy looked pleased. 'The spell worked perfectly. Right, I just need to do the flying spell –' CRASH.

Mummy and I gasped. The huge lorry behind had bumped into us. The driver looked very confused, because he couldn't see our car.

25

BANG!

CRASH!

The man was still trying to move forward – but he kept bashing us.

26

WALLOP-
CRASH-

DING!
SCRUNCH!

'Mummy Fairy!' I cried. 'We can't be invisible in a traffic jam! It's dangerous! That lorry is going to crush us.'

'Ah,' said Mummy Fairy. 'Yes, good point, Ella. Let's go.' She pressed a code on the Computawand screen – **bleep-bleep-bloop** – and said, **'Uperidoo!'**

The next moment the car whizzed straight up into the air. Then it did a big loop-the-loop like a rollercoaster.

'This is amazing!' I shouted. 'This is so cool!'

'Flyeridoo!' shouted Mummy Fairy,

and the car started flying along like a
plane. I stared out of the window at the
streets below, and all the cars and buses
and lorries in the traffic jam. Everything
looked so small. The cars were just like toy

cars, the people like tiny dolls. Even my
school looked like a toy school. There it
was, ahead in the distance.

'Have you ever flown a car before,
Mummy Fairy?' I asked.

'No, but I've flown a carpet,' she said.
'And a car is *much* easier.' She looked very

pleased with herself.

A flock of birds came near, and
Mummy Fairy quickly flew the car even
higher so we didn't bump into them. I
thought the birds looked surprised to see
us. I waved and giggled.

'Look!' said Mummy Fairy, pointing

out of the window. 'We're nearly at school. Wasn't that quick! We'd better head down, but we mustn't let anyone see us. I'll try to land behind that tree.' She pressed another code on her Computawand – **bleep–bleep–bloop**. 'Downeridoo!'

But the car didn't go down. It kept flying. It was flying and flying, away from our school, away from our town. Mummy Fairy started bashing her Computawand.

I stared out of the window. I couldn't believe it. My school was disappearing into to the distance.

'No, car!' I said. 'Go back! Back!'
'*Downeridoo!*' Mummy Fairy
shouted. '*Downeridoo!* Down, car!
DOWNERIDOO!'

The car suddenly started to go down,
and landed in a field with a *CRASH!*

Mummy Fairy and I looked at each
other. Then we stared around. All we could
see was grass and trees.

'Oops,' said Mummy Fairy. 'I don't
know how *that* happened. Maybe flying a
car isn't so easy after all.'

'Where are we?'

'Let me see . . .' Mummy Fairy looked at the sat-nav and bit her lip. 'Oh dear, we've gone FAR too far.'

We got out of the car. There weren't any roads or people or houses. All we could see was a single cow.

'We'll be really late for school.' My voice trembled but I managed not to cry. 'We'll be late and I won't get a shiny sticker and Zoe will laugh at me.'

'Zoe will NOT laugh at you,' said Mummy Fairy. She put her arms round

35

me and gave me a big hug. She wasn't
easy to hug, with her wings still scrunched
up from being in the car. 'And we will
NOT be late.'

'But, Mummy Fairy,' I
said, 'look at the car!'

The car was all crumpled up from landing in the field. It had a big dent in the back where the lorry had bashed it, and a wheel had fallen off.

'Oh dear,' said Mummy Fairy. 'That's not good. Daddy won't be pleased.'

'How will we get to school now?' I asked. 'What will we do?'

'We will –' Mummy Fairy stopped and thought.

'What?'

'We will –'

'WHAT?'

'We will walk,' said Mummy Fairy. 'With our magic legs.'

'Magic legs?' I said. 'What are magic legs?'

'They are legs that can walk extra fast. I'll do another spell. I haven't done it before, but it can't be that difficult to make magic legs.' Mummy Fairy waved her Computawand and pressed a code on the screen – *bleep–bleep–bloop*. 'Legseridoo!' she said.

At once I had a strange feeling in my legs. It was a wibbly-wobbly feeling. I looked down and gasped. 'Mummy Fairy!' I said. 'My legs have turned to jelly!'

They were all red and shiny. I looked at Mummy Fairy, and she had jelly legs too, only hers were green.

I was wobbling everywhere, and so

was Mummy Fairy. ***Wibble-wobble-wibble-wobble***.

'Oh no!' said Mummy Fairy. 'These are no good for walking!' She looked crossly at her Computawand. 'I really don't understand what went wrong.'

Suddenly I heard a snorting sound. I looked round and saw something rushing towards us. That something was the cow we had seen earlier. Only it wasn't a cow at all.

It was a bull, with two sharp horns on its
head. It was big and brown and it looked
angry.

When an angry bull is charging
towards you, you really, really don't want
jelly legs.

'Mummy Fairy!'
I yelled. 'Watch
out!

We've got jelly legs and a bull is coming!'

'He can see us!' Mummy Fairy gasped. 'The Inviseridoo spell has worn off!' She waved her Computawand and pressed a code – **bleep–bleep–bloop**. **'Inviseridoo!'** she shouted. 'Quick!'

Now we were invisible again, but the bull was still charging towards us and we still had jelly legs.

'Yikes!' said Mummy Fairy. 'It can't see us but it must be able to smell us.' She jabbed her Computawand. **'Legseridoo!'**

'Help!' I cried. 'It's getting close! Help!

42

Do another spell, Mummy Fairy.'

'Maybe this one is better.' Mummy
Fairy pressed a code on the screen –
bleep–bleep–bloop – and shouted,
'Come on, you stupid wand! Come on . . .
Rocketeridoo!'

And **WHOOSH!**

Our legs weren't jelly any more. Now
we had rocket blasters on our backs.
Just as the bull reached us, we shot high
up into the air. Mummy Fairy grabbed
my hand and I screamed: **'Aargh!'**

We did a loop-the-loop, round and round, and I shouted, 'Wheeee!' and Mummy Fairy laughed. It was very cold and very exciting and quite scary, all at once.

'You're a superhero!' said Mummy
Fairy. 'You're Super-Ella!'
    'And you're Super-Mummy-Fairy!'
I laughed.

'And look – we're here!' said Mummy Fairy.

She pointed down, and I gasped. We had whooshed so fast that we were nearly at my school.

And then I spotted something else.

'Look, Mummy Fairy! There's the traffic jam we were stuck in before. And that's what was causing it!'

Just round the corner from school a tree had fallen across the road. Some people were trying to move it, but it was very heavy.

46

'Wait a moment,' said Mummy Fairy.
'I can fix this.'

'But, Mummy Fairy, we're going
to be late,' I said. I didn't want her to
forget about my shiny sticker. We dived
down towards the tree and hovered in
the air. I could tell that Mummy Fairy
was thinking. Then she pressed a code
on her Computawand screen – *bleep-
bleep-bloop*. She waved it in a circle and
shouted, 'Whirleridoo!'

A whirlwind started to blow, round and
round. It lifted the tree right up into the air.

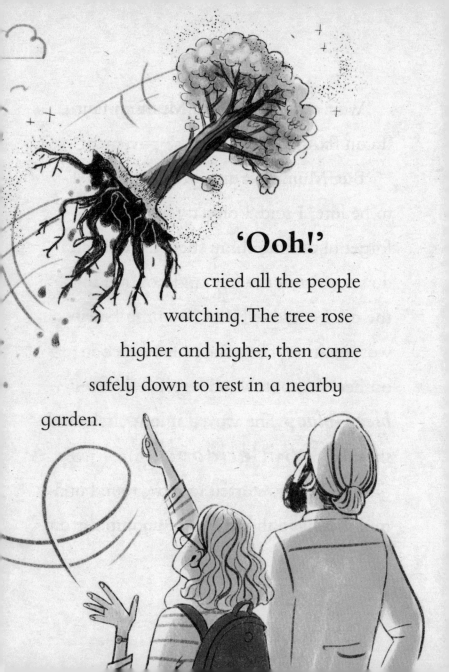

'Ooh!'

cried all the people
watching. The tree rose
higher and higher, then came
safely down to rest in a nearby
garden.

At once the traffic started moving again. All the people on the pavement cheered. One man cried, 'It's a miracle!'

Mummy Fairy looked pleased with herself. She patted her Computawand. 'Maybe I should be a traffic warden,' she said.

'Maybe,' I said, although I didn't mean it. Mummy should *not* be a traffic warden.

Together, Mummy Fairy and I floated down into the school playground. I was glad to have normal legs again. We both had sticky-uppy hair from whooshing

around in the sky, but luckily Mummy
Fairy had a hairbrush in her bag.

'All right,' she said. 'Let's go and get
that sticker.' She waved her wand, pressed
a code – *bleep-bleep-bloop* – and said,
'Stoperidoo!'

50

At once, we weren't invisible any more. We didn't have rocket blasters any more. Then Mummy Fairy said, 'Toffee apple' . . . and she wasn't Mummy Fairy any more. She was just Mummy.

Together, we walked into school and up to my classroom. None of my classmates had arrived yet. My teacher, Miss Amy, looked up and gave me a big smile.

'Hello, Ella,' she said. 'You're the first to arrive today! You get the special shiny sticker!'

She gave me a sticker with pink

sparkles, and I stuck it on my sweatshirt. I felt so, *so* happy.

'Everyone else has been stuck in a terrible traffic jam!' said Miss Amy. 'Didn't you get stuck too?'

Mummy looked at me, and I looked at Mummy.

'We did get stuck,' said Mummy. 'But then we managed to get out. We were lucky.' She winked at me. 'I'd better tell Daddy that he needs to take the car to the garage. It's *always* breaking down in the wrong place.'

Mummy kissed me and went off to work. I sat down at my desk and started doing some colouring. Then Zoe came dashing into the classroom. Her cheeks were pink and she ran in so fast she didn't see me.

'I'm first!' she said. 'Everyone else is stuck in traffic, but we left the car and ran all the way! I'm first! I'm first, Miss Amy! I'm going to get the special shiny sticker!'

'Actually,' said Miss Amy, 'Ella was first.'

Zoe went all quiet. She turned round and saw me. Her cheeks grew pinker. She looked at my sticker and her eyes went very big – then small and mean.

'How did *you* get here?' she said. And I knew she was really, really cross.

'We went a different way,' I said.

'There isn't a different way!' shouted Zoe. 'There isn't! There's just one way. And it had a traffic jam!'

'There must be,' said Miss Amy. 'Because look – Ella's here. Now sit down, Zoe, and please stop shouting.'

Zoe sat down, but she still looked grumpy. She banged her bag down on the table.

I didn't say anything else. I just carried on colouring. I thought about Mummy Fairy and the flying car. I thought about being invisible and the jelly legs and the bull and the rocket blasters. I thought about me and Mummy Fairy

saving everyone from the traffic jam, and
what Daddy would say when he saw the
car. I drew it all in my book. And I stroked
my special shiny sticker and smiled.

SPAGHETTERIDOO!
The great pasta playdate

My best friends Tom and Lenka were coming to my house on Saturday and I was so excited! At school on Friday, we made a plan for the playdate. Lenka was bringing her puppet theatre and we were going to put on a show. The story was about a princess and a prince and a scary dragon, because those are the puppets Lenka has.

Tom said he would be the scary dragon. But Lenka wanted to be the scary dragon too, and so did I. We all started to get a bit cross – until Lenka said, 'Why don't we take turns at being the scary dragon?'

Lenka is good at fixing arguments.

Then Zoe came past. She tossed her head and said, 'Your stupid playdate sounds really boring.'

Zoe always says mean things like that, which is why she is my Not-Best Friend. I ignored her, because Mummy says it is always best to ignore mean people. But then Zoe added, 'Ella's house is really weird. Her whole *family*

is weird.' And she wrinkled her nose as though she could smell something bad.

I felt really cross then. I said, 'My house is *not* weird!'

Zoe said, 'Yes it is. It's weird and strange.'

Tom said, '*You're* weird and strange, Zoe.'

Lenka and I giggled, and Tom started laughing too. Then Zoe's eyes went very small and angry and she said, 'I'm telling Miss Amy on you!'

She ran off, but I knew she wouldn't tell Miss Amy, because Miss Amy would say, 'Who started it?'

Then Tom asked, 'Are we having spaghetti at your house, Ella?' and I said, 'Of course!'

I had told Mummy lots of times that Tom and Lenka's favourite food was spaghetti, and she had promised to make it. I love spaghetti too. (Except not when it has cheese on it.)

'Yum!' said Tom. 'I'm going to bring my special spaghetti fork. It has a battery and it twirls round and round and it's awesome.'

I couldn't wait to see Tom's spaghetti

fork and I couldn't wait to put on the puppet show. It was going to be the best playdate ever!

★

On Saturday I woke up really early and gazed at my unicorn poster for a while. I love my unicorn poster. Then I got up and looked around the house.

It didn't look strange or weird – but it did look messy. So I decided to do something about it.

'Come on, Wardrobe!' I said. 'We're going to tidy up.'

Wardrobe is my magic pet wardrobe. I'm training it to do what I say. It's a bit like having a dog, except Wardrobe is more wooden than a dog and doesn't say 'Woof'.

Wardrobe followed me around the house on its little legs. I picked up books, toys and odd socks off the floor and threw them into Wardrobe. Wardrobe helped by swinging open its doors to catch things and shuffling things along with its feet.

Just when everything was tidied up, Mummy came out of her bedroom holding my little brother, Ollie. She said, 'Good morning, Ella! Good morning, Wardrobe!' And Wardrobe made a loud noise: **'Buuuuurp!'**

I said, 'Wardrobe! That's rude!'

Mummy said, 'Wardrobe sounds a bit full to me.' Then she said, 'I've bought some delicious sausages for your playdate, Ella. We can make mashed potato too.'

I stared at Mummy in shock. I said, 'But what about the spaghetti?'

Mummy stared back, then clapped her hand to her head. 'Spaghetti!' she said. 'I forgot. Well, don't worry, Ella. I'm sure we've got spaghetti.'

But when Mummy emptied the spaghetti packet into a pan, there was only one, lonely strand. It went *ping!* as it landed. Then it broke in two.

'Oh dear,' said Mummy. 'I think we need some magic.'

'Or a shop?' I said, because sometimes Mummy's magic goes a bit wrong.

67

'Nonsense!' she said. 'A spell will be much quicker.'

She stamped her feet three times, clapped her hands, wiggled her bottom and said, 'Marshmallow' . . . and **POOF!** she was a fairy, with glittery wings and a crown.

'We need some drinks too,' she said. 'What would you like?'

'Tom likes orange juice,' I said.

'Easy-peasy,' said Mummy Fairy. She pressed a code on her Computawand – *bleep–bleep–bloop* – and said,

'Orangeridoo!'

At once her face and arms turned orange.

'Mummy Fairy!' I said. 'You've gone orange!' Then I looked at *my* arms. 'So have I!'

'Weezi-weezi-weezi!' said Ollie, who had turned bright orange too.

'Oops,' said Mummy Fairy, peering at her Computawand. 'I don't know how *that* happened.'

Just then Daddy came in. His face was orange as well.

'I'm orange!' he said. 'I look like a carrot!'

'Never mind,' said Mummy Fairy. She pressed another code – **bleep-bleep-bloop** – and said, **'Normeridoo!'** At once our skin went back to normal.

'Phew,' said Daddy. 'Maybe that's enough magic for today.'

'No!' said Mummy Fairy. 'I need to make spaghetti. I promised Ella. Don't worry – spaghetti is a very easy spell.'

She pointed her Computawand at the saucepan, pressed a code – **bleep-bleep-bloop** – and said, **'Spaghetteridoo!'**

All at once spaghetti started filling up the pan. But it wasn't dried spaghetti – it was cooked spaghetti, all soft and floppy. It quickly filled the pan, spilled over the top and began piling up on the floor. It looked like slithery white worms.

'*What?*' said Daddy.

'Mummy Fairy!' I said. 'That's too much spaghetti! We only need three platefuls!'

'It's cold,' said Daddy, touching a strand. 'Cold spaghetti. Oh dear.'

'Weezi-weezi-weezi!' yelled Ollie joyfully. He grabbed some spaghetti off the floor and piled it on his head.

'Oops,' said Mummy Fairy, peering at

the spaghetti. 'I don't know how *that* happened.'

She quickly pressed a code on her Computawand, but it didn't go **bleep-bleep-bloop** like it normally does. It just went **bleep-bleep**. She tried again – but it went **bleep-bleep** again.

'Oh no! The button is stuck!' said Mummy Fairy. She jabbed at the button again. 'Come on, you silly Computawand!'

'Hurry!' said Daddy.

Spaghetti kept pouring out of the pan.

By now there was spaghetti all over the kitchen floor, and in the hall too. It was like a big, thick spaghetti carpet. Ollie was rolling around in it, laughing and kicking.

Suddenly I remembered something I had read in one of Mummy's fairy magazines.

'Mummy Fairy!' I said. 'You can use honey if a button on your Computawand gets stuck.'

'Honey!' said Mummy Fairy. 'Of course. Well done, Ella.'

She grabbed some honey from the cupboard and spooned a tiny bit on to the stuck button. At last it worked. She pressed the code – **bleep-bleep-bloop** – and shouted, 'Stoperidoo!'

The spaghetti stopped pouring out of the pan and we all looked at each other.

'Well, at least it's stopped,' said Mummy Fairy.

'Yes,' said Daddy. 'But I've never seen so much spaghetti in my life!'

There was spaghetti *everywhere*. It was on the worktop and the floor – some was

even hanging from the
lightshade.

'What shall we do
with it?' I said. 'We can't
eat it. Ollie has rolled
and dribbled all over it.'

Mummy Fairy looked
at her Computawand. 'I
could do another spell,'
she said.

'Or I could get the
wheelbarrow,' said
Daddy.

'Yes,' said Mummy Fairy. 'Maybe that's a better idea. Toffee apple!' And at once she was a normal mummy again.

Daddy got his wheelbarrow and we carted all the spaghetti into the garden. It took lots of trips, backwards and forwards. We made a pile and covered it with leaves. Daddy said that when it dried out we could have a bonfire.

At last we went inside, puffing – and the doorbell rang. It was Lenka and her mummy, holding the puppet theatre.

'Are we too early?' said Lenka's mummy.

'No!' said Mummy. 'Perfect timing! Come in.'

Lenka and her mummy came in and showed us the puppet theatre, and Mummy made some coffee.

Then suddenly Lenka's mummy gasped. 'Goodness!' she said. 'What an amazing costume!'

Mummy and Daddy and I turned round, and we gasped too. Ollie had come into the kitchen *covered* in spaghetti. I realized what had happened – he had gone into the garden and rolled in the spaghetti pile. And there he was, all wrapped up in spaghetti like a big round meatball.

Lenka and her mummy looked so surprised that I felt worried. I thought Lenka would think that my house was really strange and weird.

'Is that real spaghetti?' she said, and her mummy laughed.

'Of course it's not real spaghetti, Lenka. No one has that much spaghetti!'

'Actually, I think Ollie's nappy needs changing,' said Daddy quickly. 'I'll do it.' He picked him up and took him upstairs.

Then the doorbell rang again, and it was Tom.

While our mummies all drank coffee, Tom, Lenka and I set up the puppet theatre in the hall, next to the wardrobe, which had been tidying up downstairs. We were just getting the puppets out when there was a loud noise: **'Buuuuurp!'**

Lenka and Tom looked astonished.

'Ella,' said Tom. 'Did that wardrobe just . . . burp?'

'How could a wardrobe burp?' I said. I tried to

laugh – but I felt
worried again.

Then Lenka said,
'Your house isn't like
anyone else's, Ella.
It's really cool.'

'Yes,' said Tom.
'It's cool.'

Happiness whooshed through me. I knew our house was different from other people's – and now I felt proud of it.

Then Daddy came downstairs holding Ollie. All the spaghetti was gone. He winked at me and said, 'I'm going out to buy some more spaghetti. Who wants ice cream?' and Tom and Lenka shouted, 'Yay!'

★

That afternoon, after Tom and Lenka had gone home, I sat in the kitchen drawing pictures of everything we'd done. I drew the puppets and Tom's twirling spaghetti

84

fork. Then I drew our kitchen covered in spaghetti and I started to laugh. I showed my picture to Mummy and she laughed too.

I said, 'Our house isn't like anyone else's, is it?' and she said, 'No, Ella, it certainly isn't. And we are not like anyone else.'

I drew a picture of Wardrobe and coloured it in. Then I said, 'Zoe thinks we're strange and weird. But Tom and Lenka think we're cool.'

Mummy kissed me on the head and said, 'What do you think we are?'

I thought for a bit, and then I said, 'I think we're cool.'

'I think we're cool too,' said Mummy. 'I think we're super-cool.'

'We're super-super-*super*-cool,' I said. And I looked up at her and smiled.

TWIRLERIDOO!
Sheep don't dance, do they?

One day I was watching Mummy having her magic lesson with Fenella on FairyTube. She was learning about the Rainbow Effect.

The Rainbow Effect is very powerful and mysterious. When there is a rainbow in the sky, fairies have to be careful because their spells are extra strong and very hard to control.

That's why there's a Rainbow App on every Computawand. The app tells you when a rainbow is coming. All fairies have them except Granny. She doesn't like apps or Computawands. She says, 'Just look at the sky, dear.'

Mummy finished her lesson and I said, 'I wish *I* could have magic lessons.'

Mummy smiled and said, 'You can't have magic lessons yet, Ella. But guess what? You're going to start dancing lessons!'

'Yay!' I said, excited. 'Dancing!' I started
to dance around the room, whirling my
arms.

'Weezi-weezi-
weezi!' shouted Ollie. He
whirled his arms too, and
knocked his breadsticks
all over the floor.

I couldn't wait for dancing lessons. I went shopping with Mummy and we bought pink ballet shoes. I wanted to buy a pink tutu with a frilly skirt, but Mummy said, 'Maybe another time.'

When we arrived for the first lesson, there were lots of children there. One of them was Zoe, my Not-Best Friend from next door.

'Oh look,' said Mummy. 'Zoe does dancing too. That's good, isn't it?'

Sometimes Mummy doesn't understand about Zoe. It wasn't good – it was bad, because Zoe is always mean to me. But luckily she didn't see me. She was in the front row, doing very high jumps with pointy toes.

I tried to copy her – but I fell over.

'Never mind!' said Mummy. 'It's never easy when you start, Ella. But keep trying. I know you can do it. Have fun!'

Then Zoe saw me. She came over and said in her mean voice, 'Oh, Ella, *you're* here. I'm really good at dancing. I've been coming for ages. I bet you're really bad.'

'I bet I'm *not*,' I said.

I decided to try my best at dancing. I watched the teacher, Miss Evans, very hard. We did good toes and naughty toes. We did arms up and down. We did

a special jump called a cat jump. I said,
'Meow!' when I jumped, because it made
me feel like a cat.

At the end of the lesson Miss Evans

said, 'We have a special treat today. Zoe's cousin Sally is here. Sally is a real grown-up ballerina and she is going to show us her dancing.'

Sally was wearing a lovely swishy skirt. She told us how she practised dancing every day. Then she danced on her tiptoes. She did twirls, round and round. We all clapped and cheered. I wanted to do a twirl so, *so* badly, but I didn't know how.

On our way out we all thanked Sally for showing us her dancing.

I said, 'I wish I could do a twirl.'

'I'm sure you will one day!' said Sally.
'Keep trying!'

But Zoe was standing nearby. She
came close so no one could hear, then said,
'*You'll* never do a twirl, Ella. You can't even
point your toes properly. You're rubbish
at dancing.' And she laughed her horrible
laugh.

★

That weekend it was very sunny. Mummy,
Ollie and I went for a picnic with Aunty Jo.
We drove out into the countryside and sat

on some grass. All the fields around us had animals in them. One had sheep, one had pigs and one had two horses. I gave some carrots to the horses over the fence. I tried to give a carrot to a sheep, but it ran away.

'Have a sandwich, Ella,' called Mummy, and I hurried back to the picnic rug. But, just as I took a bite, it started raining.

'Oh no!' I said. 'What about our picnic?'

'Don't worry!' said Aunty Jo. 'Fairy to the rescue!'

She looked around to check that no one could see us. Then she stamped her feet three times, clapped her hands, wiggled her bottom and said, 'Sherbet lemon' . . . and **POOF!** she was a fairy with shining wings and a beautiful diamond crown.

She held out her Computawand, pressed a code – *bleep-bleep-bloop* – and shouted, *'Umbrelleridoo!'*

Straight away a great big floating umbrella appeared above us. It had green and white stripes and was so enormous it kept the rain off us all. Aunty Jo is very good at magic.

While we ate our picnic, I told Aunty Jo Fairy all about my dancing lessons. I even got my bag out of the car and showed her my pink ballet shoes. I told her how much I wanted to do a twirl. Then Aunty Jo Fairy said, 'You need the Twirleridoo spell!'

At once I felt excited. A Twirleridoo spell sounded really cool!

But Mummy said, 'Jo, Ella needs to learn dancing through hard work, not through magic.'

'Oh, I know,' said Aunty Jo Fairy. 'Of course. Hard work, and all that. But why

100

don't I just *show* Ella the Twirleridoo spell?
Look, the rain has stopped.'

Aunty Jo Fairy walked into the middle
of the field, pointed her Computawand
at herself, pressed a code – **bleep–bleep–
bloop** – and shouted, **'Twirleridoo!'**

I gasped, because ballet shoes appeared
on Aunty Jo Fairy's feet and she started
whizzing round on one leg. She was
much faster than Sally the ballerina.
Every time she slowed down she shouted,
'Twirleridoo!' and started twirling
again.

I clapped and cried,
'Amazing!' I wanted to
ask if I could do it too, but I knew
Mummy would say no.

Just then I glanced up at the sky. It
was blue again. The sun was out and
there was a rainbow. At first I thought:
A rainbow – yay! Then I suddenly
remembered about the
Rainbow Effect.
'Mummy!' I said
quickly. 'Look out!
There's a rainbow!'

'A *rainbow*?' Mummy looked up. 'My Rainbow App said it would be tomorrow. Jo!' she called out. 'Watch out! Rainbow!'

'Aunty Jo Fairy!' I shouted. 'Rainbow!'

But Aunty Jo Fairy couldn't hear either of us. She was saying, **'Twirleridoo!'** and whizzing round.

Mummy ran towards Aunty Jo Fairy, pointing at the sky and yelling, 'Jo! **RAINBOW!**'

At last Aunty Jo Fairy heard. She stopped saying, 'Twirleridoo,' and slowed down. 'It's fine,' she panted. 'No

104

harm done. Everything's fine,
everything's normal.'
But everything wasn't fine
and everything wasn't normal.
'Look!' I gasped. '*Look!*'
I was staring at the sheep
in the nearest field. They were
all twirling round on one foot,
just like Aunty Jo Fairy. They
were wearing purple ballet
shoes and saying, **'Baaa!'**
while they twirled, as
though they didn't

understand what was going on.

'Dancing *sheep*?' said Mummy when she saw them. 'Jo, what have you *done*?'

'It's not my fault!' said Aunty Jo Fairy. 'It's the Rainbow Effect.'

'Look, dancing pigs!' I said, pointing to the next field. The pigs were twirling too, in little piggy ballet shoes, only theirs were blue. **'Weezi-weezi-weezi!'** said Ollie, and he pointed at the horses.

They were both twirling and tossing their manes. All the animals were dancing in different coloured ballet shoes.

Even the squirrels in the tree were twirling round on the branches and looking very surprised.

I couldn't stop laughing, but Mummy looked worried.

'The Rainbow Effect is very special and powerful,' she said. 'It can't be undone with a spell. We'll just have to wait for it to wear off.'

Just then, a farmer in an old brown jacket came walking across the grass.

'Oh no!' said Mummy. 'I hope he doesn't notice anything wrong.'

But as soon as the farmer looked into the first field, he stopped. 'What's happened to my sheep?' he demanded. 'They look like whirligigs!' Then he saw the pigs. 'What's happened to my pigs?' he gasped. 'They're dancing too! Pigs aren't supposed to dance!'

'Er . . . maybe they got bored?' said Aunty Jo Fairy.

Then the farmer saw the horses, and I thought he was going to fall over with

shock. One of the horses was holding the other horse by its hooves and they were both twirling round.

'Dapple!' shouted the farmer. 'Beauty! What do you think you're doing? You're not blooming ballerinas – you're *horses*.'

'I think they're stopping,' said Mummy after a moment, and it was true.

Gradually all the ballet shoes disappeared. The sheep started eating grass again, like normal sheep. The pigs started rooting around in the mud. The two horses trotted off.

I was sad – I had loved watching the dancing animals.

'**Awayeridoo!**' said Aunty Jo Fairy, pointing her Computawand at the floating umbrella, and it disappeared.

The farmer's mouth fell open. 'What's going on?' he said. 'Are you from the telly?'

'No,' said Aunty Jo Fairy. 'We're fairies.'

'Aunty Jo Fairy!' I said, shocked. 'You told him!'

'Yes,' she said, winking at me. 'But

he won't remember.' Then she said,
'Blueberry pie!' and at once she was just
Aunty Jo again.

Then Mummy took some Fairy
Dust out of her bag and
threw it over the farmer.
For about ten seconds
he was completely still.
He had sort of gone
to sleep. Then . . .

'Go!' said Mummy,
and he woke up.

He smiled politely at us all. 'Hello,' he said. 'Are you having a nice picnic? Did you see that lovely rainbow?'

'Oh yes,' said Mummy. 'We certainly did.'

★

When I arrived at my next dancing lesson, I kept thinking about the twirling sheep. I decided I would try to twirl exactly like them.

As I put on my ballet shoes, I noticed that they looked strange. They were gleaming as if a rainbow was shining on

them. I didn't understand why, but I
put them on and went into the class.
I stepped on to one foot and started to
turn – and just for fun I said, very quietly,
'Twirleridoo!'

To my surprise I did a perfect twirl!
Then another one!

I couldn't understand how I was
twirling. Then I looked down at my shiny
rainbow shoes again and realized that it
was the Rainbow Effect! There was some
left in my shoes!

'Look at Ella!' cried a boy named

Callum. 'She's really good!'

I twirled round again and again. My
legs were just doing it by themselves!

I didn't know how, but they were! I could see Zoe staring furiously at me, but I didn't care. I felt like a real ballerina.

'How come you can do that, Ella?' she shouted. 'You're only a beginner!'

I hoped my shoes would stay magic forever, but already the rainbow light was fading. I did one last twirl – and then it was gone. The magic was over. The next time I stepped on to one foot, it didn't know how to twirl any more. It felt all heavy and strange.

'Do it again!' said Callum.

'I can't,' I said.

Just then Miss Evans came in. Everyone rushed up and told her how I had been twirling.

'Show me, Ella,' she said with a smile, but I said, 'I've forgotten how.'

'Never mind,' she said kindly. 'I'm sure you'll learn again.'

'I'm sure she won't,' said Zoe, looking at me with her small, angry eyes. 'Anyway, her twirls weren't that good.'

'Zoe,' said Miss Evans. 'That is not polite.'

She looked at Zoe quite hard. The whole room was silent and Zoe turned pink.

'In this class,' said Miss Evans, 'we say *kind* things to our classmates.'

Then we started our lesson and I tried my hardest. We didn't do twirls but we did snowflakes. I tried to be a very light snowflake – except I was too busy looking at Miss Evans and crashed into Callum by mistake. He said, 'Snow*flake*!

Not snow*storm*!' and we all laughed.

While we were getting ready to go home, Zoe stayed in the middle of the room doing twirls. I remembered what Miss Evans had told us about saying kind things. Zoe isn't a nice person but she is still good at twirls. So I went up to her and said, 'You twirl really well, Zoe! You're just as good as a sheep.'

As soon as I said it I realized I shouldn't have said 'sheep'. Zoe stared at me with her tiny, furious eyes. She shouted, 'A *sheep*? Miss Evans, Ella called me a sheep!'

Everyone started to laugh. I felt hot and bothered.

'I meant it in a *good* way!' I said. 'I was being nice!' But I could tell that Zoe didn't believe me.

'Ella called me a sheep!' she wailed, and she started crying loudly. (Though I think she was pretending.)

'Ella,' said Miss Evans, coming over. 'Why did you call Zoe a sheep? I'm very disappointed.'

I felt as if I might cry myself. I didn't want Miss Evans to be disappointed, but I didn't know how to reply. Then, suddenly, I heard Mummy's voice saying, 'I can explain!'

'Really?' said Miss Evans.

'Oh yes,' said Mummy. 'Zoe, Ella didn't

mean to offend you. The truth is . . . we once saw a whole field of wonderful, graceful dancing sheep.'

I gazed at her, astonished. Was she going to tell everyone about Twirleridoo and being a fairy?

But then Mummy added, 'In a book. Of course.' And she winked at me.

★

In the car on the way home, I told Mummy about my twirls and took my ballet shoes out of my bag. I wanted to see if there were any shiny bits of the

Rainbow Effect left in them, even a tiny speck. But they were just normal pink ballet shoes.

'I wish I could still twirl,' I said. 'I wish I still had the Rainbow Effect on my shoes. When I'm grown up I'll do the Twirleridoo spell every day.'

'I'm sure you will,' said Mummy, nodding. She drove on for a bit, then said, 'But that's a long time to wait. What about for now?'

I thought about trying to twirl. I thought about Sally whizzing round.

124

I thought about how she practises dancing every day. And I decided I wanted to be like her.

'For now,' I said, 'I'll practise twirling every day until I can do it.'

'Good idea, Ella,' said Mummy. 'That's my girl.' And she looked over at me, and we both smiled.

GLITCHERIDOO!
A unicorn in the kitchen

One day I was in the kitchen reading Mummy's Spell Book. It was written long ago by the Old, Old Fairies. Every fairy has one, even though lots of them use their Fairy Apps now. I was reading about Bad Magic. If you try to use magic to be lazy or mean or cruel, it is called Bad Magic and it won't turn out well.

Mummy was making a cup of coffee.

'Mummy,' I said. 'When I'm a grown-up fairy, I'll never use Bad Magic.'

'Good girl, Ella,' she said, smiling at me.

Then Aunty Jo arrived. She was very excited. She said, 'Have you heard about the new, super-cool Fairy App? It's called Auto-Spell! Let's all watch the advert!'

Aunty Jo loves buying apps for her Computawand. Mummy says most of them are a waste of money as they always glitch. (That means they get stuck or go wrong.) But, even so, she opened

FairyTube on her laptop and we all watched the advert for Auto-Spell. A fairy was holding her Computawand while her bicycle mended itself. She smiled and said, '*Auto-Spell is the first Fairy App that can read your mind. It casts the spell you need even before you know you need it! Buy Auto-Spell now!*'

Aunty Jo said, 'This will make magic so easy. I'm going to buy it.'

Mummy stared at the screen for a bit. Then she said, 'I'm going to buy it too.'

I was so excited. We were going to have a new, super-cool app!

★

When Auto-Spell arrived, it looked like a tiny gold coin. It wasn't like a normal app that

you can just buy from the app store.
Mummy fitted it into a special slot in
her Computawand. She screwed the
panel shut and turned it on. Then she
stamped her feet three times, clapped
her hands, wiggled her bottom and said,
'Marshmallow' . . . and **POOF!** she
was a fairy.

Meanwhile I was looking at the
instruction booklet. It had lots of pictures
of fairies holding cups of tea and
watching lawnmowers working. The
writing said:

Auto-Spell

Welcome to Auto-Spell! Simply relax and think your normal thoughts. Auto-Spell will read your mind and cast all the spells you wish for.

1. 2. 3.

I said, 'Mummy Fairy, shall I read out the instructions?' but Mummy Fairy said, 'Don't worry, Ella. I expect I can work it out as I go.'

Mummy Fairy never reads instruction booklets, but I like looking at them and colouring in the pictures.

Mummy Fairy came over to the kitchen table and the chair pulled itself out.

'Thank you, Auto-Spell!' she said, sitting down. Then the teapot lifted itself up and poured her some tea. Mummy Fairy looked pleased.

'Isn't this wonderful?' she said to Daddy. 'Tea was exactly what I wanted.' Then the cornflakes packet rose into the air and poured me a big bowl of cornflakes.

'Thank you, Mummy Fairy!' I said. 'Thank you, Auto-Spell!'

I wanted a nice big breakfast because I was going to the park with Tom and Lenka. Tom's dad was going to teach us some football skills.

At that moment Aunty Jo came in through the back door. She was breathing hard, as though she had been running.

'Have you got the Auto-Spell app?' she asked. 'Is it any good? Mine hasn't arrived yet.'

'Yes!' said Mummy Fairy. 'It's brilliant! It's reading my mind. It's doing everything I want.'

Just then a big plate of pancakes covered in chocolate sauce and marshmallows landed on the table.

'Mmm!' I said. 'Thank you, Mummy Fairy! Thank you, Auto-Spell!'

Mummy Fairy looked puzzled. 'I didn't want pancakes,' she said, just as a huge strawberry milkshake with a stripy straw appeared in front of me.

'Strawberry is my favourite!' I said. 'And I love stripy straws!'

Mummy Fairy stared at me. She said, 'Ella, did you imagine me having a cup of tea just now?'

'Yes,' I said. 'You always have a cup of tea for breakfast, Mummy Fairy. And toast.'

As I said the word 'toast', a toast rack floated down towards Mummy Fairy.

It was full of toast.

Mummy Fairy gasped in horror. 'I think Auto-Spell is reading the wrong mind!' she said. 'It has tuned into Ella's mind instead of mine! I should have read the instruction booklet.'

'Tragic,' said Aunty Jo, shaking her head. 'Didn't you read the instruction booklet? I *always* do.'

'Ella, you must stop thinking of things,' said Daddy as Mummy Fairy grabbed the instructions. 'Do you understand? Don't think about *anything*.'

'OK, Daddy,' I said. 'I'll try.'

But it's hard not to think about anything. Just then, there was a neighing sound from the hall. A unicorn was standing at the kitchen door, looking in at us. It had a fluffy white mane and its horn was glittering in the sunlight.

'Ella, did you wish for a unicorn?' asked Mummy Fairy.

'I always wish for a unicorn,' I said. 'All the time.'

The unicorn came into the kitchen and I put my arms round it. It was so soft and gentle that I kissed it. I felt

so happy. I had a real unicorn!

Then a chocolate fountain appeared in the middle of the kitchen.

'Ella!' exclaimed Aunty Jo. 'Stop thinking!'

I tried my hardest not to think about anything – but I couldn't. Soon there were lots of kittens all over the kitchen, mewing and licking their paws. There was a merry-go-round in the garden and I had a lolly in my hand.

Ollie was sitting in his high chair watching the kittens. He banged his spoon on his tray and said, 'Weezi-weezi-weezi!'

I thought to myself, *I wish Ollie could speak properly*, just like I always do.

Then Ollie said, 'Goodness! I can talk now. Hello, Ella. You're an awesome big sister.'

I clapped my hand over my mouth. I had made Ollie talk!

'Enough!' said Daddy, looking shocked. 'We have to stop this *now*!'

'I'm trying to remove the app,' said

Mummy Fairy, 'but I can't get it out!'
She was trying to open the panel on her
Computawand with a screwdriver, but it
seemed to be stuck.

Suddenly Aunty Jo screamed. A huge,
scary eye was looking in at us through the
kitchen window.

'Ella!' said
Aunty Jo.
'Don't wish for
a dinosaur!'

'I didn't!' I said.

'Dinosaur!' cried Ollie joyfully. 'I love dinosaurs!' He waved his hands at the dinosaur, and I gasped.

'Mummy Fairy! I think the app is reading *Ollie's* mind now!'

At that moment there was a roaring sound, and a little red steam train came puffing into the kitchen.

'Ella, I think you're right!' said Daddy.

'I'm a train driver,' said Ollie. 'That's my train. *Choo choo!*'

But then the train turned into a big red
snake and we all screamed.

'Who wished for a snake?' said Daddy.

'Nobody!' I said.

Snow started falling from the ceiling,
and thunder rumbled in the sky above.
The snake hissed. The dinosaur batted the

window with its head and roared angrily at us, and I shivered in fright.

'The app is glitching!' said Aunty Jo. 'It's gone wrong.'

Ollie said, 'Everything's so scary! I don't understand! I want my teddy!' Then he started crying: **_'Waaaah!'_**

Mummy Fairy was still struggling with her Computawand. 'Quick,' she said to Aunty Jo. 'We need the Glitcheridoo spell!'

Aunty Jo quickly stamped her feet three times, clapped her hands, wiggled her bottom and said, 'Sherbet lemon.' At once she was a fairy, with big, strong, shiny wings. She pressed a code – *bleep-bleep-bloop* – then pointed her Computawand at the snake and shouted, 'Glitcheridoo!' Straight away it disappeared. Then she made the dinosaur disappear.

'Thank goodness!' said Daddy.

But then a great big tentacle came through the kitchen door. There was an octopus in the hall! It was huge and slimy and it was coming towards us!

'The app is still glitching!' cried Aunty Jo Fairy. 'Glitcheridoo!'

She quickly made the octopus disappear, but the next minute a sea lion appeared in the sink. The floor started swaying backwards and forwards and the sky turned pink.

'Hurry!' said Aunty Jo Fairy to Mummy Fairy. 'Everything is very strange!'

At last Mummy Fairy got the panel on her Computawand open and pulled out the gold coin.

There was a sort of *crash!* and a flash of light – then everything was quiet. All the strange things had disappeared. The world was back to normal. We were all breathing hard, looking at each other.

'Well!' said Mummy Fairy at last. 'I didn't expect that!'

I looked at the app in her hand. It was such a tiny gold coin, but it had created so much trouble.

Suddenly I realized what had happened.

I said, 'I think the app is Bad Magic. It's using magic to be lazy. That's why it went wrong.'

Aunty Jo Fairy looked very surprised. 'Ella, how do you know about Bad Magic?' she asked. 'That's very grown up.'

'I read about it in Mummy Fairy's Spell Book,' I told her.

'Well, I think you're right,' said Aunty Jo

152

Fairy. 'Auto-Spell is Bad Magic. I'll send my app back.'

'I'm sending mine back too,' said Mummy Fairy. 'I'm going to complain.'

'Weezi-weezi-weezi!' said Ollie, banging his spoon. I was so glad he was back to normal that I went to give him a great big hug.

The only thing I was sad about was my unicorn. I had loved it so much, and now it was gone.

'Can I have a unicorn one day?' I asked. 'A real unicorn?'

'Maybe,' said Mummy Fairy. 'When you're a grown-up fairy.'

I decided that the minute I was a grown-up fairy I would have a unicorn. And ten kittens. And ice cream every day.

★

Two weeks later, Mummy came into the kitchen holding her laptop. She said, 'Look at this, Ella.'

She was watching Fairy News on FairyTube. A fairy was looking very serious as she said, '*The new Auto-Spell app has been banned. It is Bad Magic and it has*

caused a lot of trouble. If you've bought the Auto-Spell app, please send it back to the Fairy Store, and you will get your money back.'

Mummy pressed PAUSE. She said, 'You were right, Ella. Well done!' Then she said, 'Maybe you will invent a Fairy App one day. A *good* Fairy App.'

I thought about the Fairy App I would invent one day. It would be very useful and clever. Maybe it would give food to hungry people. Or maybe it would stop people having accidents.

Then I remembered the pink sky and

the thunder and the dinosaur's scary eye.
I looked at Mummy and I said, 'If I invent
a Fairy App, it will definitely not glitch.
Ever.'

Mummy laughed and said, 'Certainly
not! No glitches for Ella!'

'**Weezi-weezi-weezi!**' said
Ollie, as if he was agreeing.

'That's right, Ollie,' I said. 'No glitches
for me.' And I looked up at Mummy and
smiled.

TEST YOUR
Fairy Skills

Turn the page for lots of fun activities!

You can find all these activities at
www.puffin.co.uk/mummyfairy,
where you can print them out and test
your fairy skills again and again!

BAGSERIDOO!

Design your own fairy handbag!

What do you think a fairy would keep inside her handbag? Write a list here! There are a few ideas to start you off.

Computawand

Fairy Dust

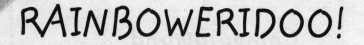

RAINBOWERIDOO!

Make your own rainbow appear with this fun activity – and don't forget to add glitter to make it look extra special!

★ Make sure you ask a grown-up to help you with cutting out.

WHAT YOU NEED:
★ A paper plate
★ Scissors
★ Paint or crayons
★ Glue (optional)
★ Cotton wool (optional)
★ Glitter (optional)

WHAT TO DO:

1 With a grown-up's help, cut the paper plate in half. Next, cut out a semicircle from the middle of the plate, to get a rainbow shape.

2 Use your paint or crayons to colour in stripes for your rainbow. Follow the curve of the plate, and you can start from the top or bottom curve. Ask a grown-up to draw lines to follow if that makes it easier.

3 The colours of a rainbow are (starting from the top): red, orange, yellow, green, blue, purple and violet (light purple). But don't worry if you don't have all these colours. A magical rainbow can have any colours you like, in any order!

4 If you like, you can glue bits of cotton wool to the bottom of your rainbow, for the clouds.

5 Add glitter to your rainbow to show that it's full of rainbow magic! Next time you see a rainbow in the sky, watch out for anything unusual happening on your street or in your town. It might be a sign that rainbow magic is really happening . . .

FINDERIDOO!

Can you spot these words

in the word search?

(Answers on page 167.)

APP

GLITCH

RAINBOW

SPAGHETTI

SPARKLE

SPELL BOOK

UMBRELLA

UNICORN

M	Y	D	I	F	C	Z	F	J	A	C	R
I	U	X	K	V	L	T	P	I	L	C	T
I	T	T	E	H	G	A	P	S	L	X	P
K	W	U	W	P	L	S	F	Y	E	C	W
E	O	F	N	F	I	W	L	W	R	O	W
J	W	O	A	I	T	Y	X	P	B	L	X
K	K	P	B	Y	C	V	N	N	M	Z	T
R	P	O	P	L	H	O	I	Y	U	H	J
K	D	F	O	I	L	A	R	C	I	J	L
G	S	V	Q	K	R	E	W	N	T	O	L
C	V	H	Q	O	N	C	P	T	V	A	C
S	P	A	R	K	L	E	S	S	H	W	B

165

WISHERIDOO!

If you had the Auto-Spell app, what would you wish for? A unicorn, like Ella – or something else? Draw your wishes here!

ANSWERS

FINDERIDOO!

M	Y	D	I	F	C	Z	F	J	A	C	R
I	U	X	K	V	L	T	P	I	L	C	T
I	T	T	E	H	G	A	P	S	L	X	P
K	W	U	W	P	L	S	F	Y	E	C	W
E	O	F	N	F	I	W	L	W	R	O	W
J	W	O	A	I	T	Y	X	P	B	L	X
K	K	P	B	Y	C	V	N	N	M	Z	T
R	P	O	P	L	H	O	I	Y	U	H	J
K	D	F	O	I	L	A	R	C	I	J	L
G	S	V	Q	K	R	E	W	N	T	O	L
C	V	H	Q	O	N	C	P	T	V	A	C
S	P	A	R	K	L	E	S	S	H	W	B

167

ABOUT SOPHIE KINSELLA

Sophie Kinsella is a bestselling author and the adventures of Ella and Mummy Fairy are her first stories for children. Her books for grown-ups have sold over forty million copies worldwide and have been translated into more than forty languages. They include the Shopaholic series and other titles such as *Can You Keep a Secret?*, *The Undomestic Goddess*, *My Not So Perfect Life*, *Surprise Me*, *I Owe You One*, and *Finding Audrey* for young adults.

You can find out more about
Sophie's books on her website:
www.sophiekinsella.co.uk